Sam Allen

MIRRORS

AUSTIN MACAULEY PUBLISHERS
LONDON · CAMBRIDGE · NEW YORK · SHARJAH

Copyright © Sam Allen 2025

All rights reserved. No part of this publication may be reproduced, distributed, or transmitted in any form or by any means, including photocopying, recording, or other electronic or mechanical methods, without the prior written permission of the publisher, except in the case of brief quotations embodied in critical reviews and certain other non-commercial uses permitted by copyright law. For permission requests, write to the publisher.

Any person who commits any unauthorized act in relation to this publication may be liable to criminal prosecution and civil claims for damages.

This is a work of fiction. Names, characters, businesses, places, events, locales, and incidents are either the products of the author's imagination or used in a fictitious manner. Any resemblance to actual persons, living or dead, or actual events is purely coincidental.

Ordering Information
Quantity sales: Special discounts are available on quantity purchases by corporations, associations, and others. For details, contact the publisher at the address below.

Publisher's Cataloging-in-Publication data
Allen, Sam
Mirrors

ISBN 9798886939262 (Paperback)
ISBN 9798886939873 (Hardback)
ISBN 9798886939880 (ePub e-book)

Library of Congress Control Number: 2024921786

www.austinmacauley.com/us

First Published 2025
Austin Macauley Publishers LLC
40 Wall Street, 33rd Floor, Suite 3302
New York, NY 10005
USA

mail-usa@austinmacauley.com
+1 (646) 5125767

Chapter I

On her last birthday, Katrina received a present and stuck it in the closet, where it remained neatly concealed, as a proper secret should. It would have stayed that way forever if it had not been for the mirror.

When first presented with the gift, it made her feel like the epitome of words she often used to describe others who wore such outfits.

Cheap. Dirty. Scandalous.

Most of all, being religious and raised on the sermons of Jesus Christ, the gift made her feel like *a wolf in sheep's clothing.*

She believed that reality TV stars, models, gold diggers, and attention-seeking teens dressed this way for only one purpose: to get something they didn't have. Utilizing a false front of beauty, they employed lascivious methods to reach the top, masking their true intentions all the way up.

The mirror, however, had a different opinion altogether. It rested against a wall in the corner of her closet, always loitering, like a hungry vagrant on the sidewalk of a strip mall, demanding that she give something even when she said there was not anything to offer. She was just smalltown, Bible-studying Katrina who had nothing to hide and no one else to be. But the mirror insisted otherwise.

This insistence began when the dress arrived in her closet. She had placed the slinky piece of cloth in the back of a cubby, but somehow—despite insisting to herself that she didn't do it—the dress ended up on the floor, facing the mirror. *A stupid little dress.* That's all it was. A silly piece of fabric. *A slutty, despicable garment that could lead to a life-ending sexually transmitted disease.*

Katrina looked into the rearview mirror of her mid-sized SUV and focused on her make-up, attempting to wipe these thoughts from her mind. She didn't want to admit it, but deep down, she knew the dress had become an addiction—if being addicted to thoughts were even possible. What scared her now was the incursion these thoughts had made into the physical universe. Instead of it being solely in her head, she had begun holding the dress to the mirror at night, imagining who she would be in it. The tight, elastic cloth painted onto the contours of her body, leaving just enough room for the imagination of those who laid eyes on her. But that was not who she was. She was nobody, and nothing rolled up into one, and that *one* needed to finish putting on her gosh-darn mascara before walking into work.

She couldn't be late. The boss was a real stickler when it came to schedule and appearance. He didn't want his employees to give the wrong impression to their customers. *Be conservative.* That was his command. Nude lipstick, light eye make-up, and a drab brown skirt with a tucked-in pressed white shirt that revealed nothing. The whole get-up was a few decades out of sync with the world, but so was the rest of this town.

She had grown up and lived her entire life here. Her fondest memories were those connected to the bank where she now worked. As a young girl, every other Friday, her daddy would bring her to the bank and together they would cash his measly paycheck. Afterward, he would take her to one of the town's three sit-down restaurants to celebrate another week of paying the bills and staying afloat. And that was about all he ever managed to do until the Man above decided it was time to cash in for good. At eighteen, fresh out of high school, without a dime to her name, she walked away from her alcoholic mother and their trailer and into the one place that still felt like home, where she asked for a job. The bank owner, Dan Stratham, who had watched her grow up, quickly obliged and even sweetened the pot by covering the first and last month's rent in a newly renovated apartment. For this, she was grateful and rewarded his generosity with fifteen years of dedicated service.

Neither his old-fashioned way of doing business nor the dress code bothered her much. The schedule was 9–5 without a minute of wiggle room. There was no such thing as leaving fifteen minutes early for a dinner date.

No cell phones or personal electronic devices were allowed in the building, and he never wanted to hear the word social media. TikTok was the sound a clock makes and nothing else. If his bank were ever to appear on any online platform containing dancing humans or animals, he would hunt down the one responsible and not only fire them but call down the full arm of the law until he owned each of their earthly possessions.

Notwithstanding this small handful of eccentricities, Dan was a pretty nice guy. "Good morning, Mr. Stratham, how was your weekend?" Katrina said, offering him a warm smile as she held the door.

She had arrived five minutes before and waited in the car until 8:59 a.m., when he drove up. This had been her routine for well over a decade.

"It was fantastic, Katrina. I went fishin' with the kids, Church on Sunday and caught the Bears game on the tube right after. Even squeezed in some long, overdue lawn work. All in all—a well-rounded weekend. You?" he said, turning his head toward her as he walked behind the counter to his office.

"Quite wonderful, thank you. After Church, I spent the day on my charity project, helping the children with special needs and—" she said, ready to drone on more about the project.

"Good stuff, Katrina, good stuff," he said distractedly before closing the door in her face.

His dismissal didn't offend her. She knew him better than he knew himself. Small talk ended after ninety seconds of entering the building, and it was 9:02 a.m. The day had begun, but all she could think about was how it would end.

Chapter II

Katrina stepped out of the bank and into her car at 5:02 p.m. She then drove nine minutes to her apartment, parked, and was inside her bedroom, standing in front of the mirror, by 5:11 p.m. Draped over one finger was a flimsy black dress; its reflection shimmered as light from the ceiling fixture bounced off pearly beads that were embedded in the fabric.

It couldn't hurt to try it on once.

She stripped to her underwear with the dress still looped around one finger. The mirror's reflection of the chic, dangling garment swayed back and forth as if laughing at and mocking the padded bra and full-coverage panties that stuck like oversized bandages to the most private sections of her body. She owned no strapless lingerie or thong underwear. Tonight, it would be the dress and nothing else.

Katrina reached one hand back and unclasped her bra. She used the other hand to tug her panties down and then shimmied her hips until she stood naked.

Without further hesitation, she stepped into the dress and pulled it up and over the curve of her backside and swelling chest as the reflection in the mirror transformed into an image of someone she no longer recognized. She peered down at the low-cut center and back at her reflection. The mirror glowed with a sea of dazzling sparkles and shimmers. Katrina could feel satisfaction radiating from the glass and knew that if the mirror could speak, it would be purring.

Katrina, a party of one? A little voice said as an imaginary hostess ushered her away from one version of herself into an alien world of glitz and glamor. A world made of people who took what they wanted and did what was needed to get it.

The words *cheap, dirty*, and *scandalous* had been replaced by *confident, proud*, and *ambitious.*

It was time to become a wolf.

Chapter III

Tony knew she was the one when he saw her lurch through the front door. Those heels, more fitting for a Church gathering, had likely been stowaways discovered only today in a deep closet corner. Like him, she didn't belong here.

This club was not his usual stomping ground. It was the first time he had been to such a place since college, when his parents had their sights set on him as a doctor, and all he had wanted to do was travel the country in a camper van, playing rock music and smoking dope. Instead, however, his life had taken a turn on Boring Street, where he remained parked ever since, working in a small town as a pharmacist's assistant, handing out the drugs doctors prescribed. And there was a good chance this was all he would ever do. But then there were those times when he looked in the mirror and saw someone else staring back at him—another version of himself, trapped, looking for a way out. Or perhaps it was the other way around, and he was the one staring back, eye to eye with the interloper, who had somehow assumed control of his life and destiny.

"Can I get four shots?" he said, waving his hand to flag down the bartender.

"Keep it open or close it out?" the man said as he poured and lined them up with bartender ease.

"Open," Tony said without taking his eye off the woman, who had begun to spin uselessly on the dance floor.

He took back-to-back shots and stood up, leaving the other two on the counter, and walked toward her.

"Hey!" he shouted over the rave music from the speakers.

She continued to bob up and down like a water-logged apple.

"Hey!" he repeated, now an inch from her body. "Can I buy you a drink?" She recoiled instinctively and slapped him across the face.

"Wow! OK. That's an introduction," he said, shaking his head. "Can I buy you a drink?" he repeated, tilting an invisible glass with his thumb and forefinger.

She looked dazedly toward the bar. Tony nodded, pointed back toward his remaining shot glasses, and began walking, hoping she would follow. When he arrived at the counter and turned, she still stood where he left her.

"OK, whatever," he muttered and swiveled toward the bar. "I'm going to need a couple more."

Tony knocked back his shots as the bartender placed two more before him.

"Hi," said a female voice from behind him.

He spun toward the woman, and as he did so, his lips almost grazed her breasts. She was practically standing in his lap. It was her.

"Hi. Do you want to sit down or—" he said as she reached over, picked up each shot glass consecutively, and emptied them in her mouth.

"Take me to the bathroom," she said abruptly.

"Oh. Sure, I can show you. I was there earlier—in the men's, not the women's, but they are next to each other, right in the same general area, side by side, in fact," he said, aware that he was now rambling. Alcohol and pretty women made him do that.

She raised her eyebrows.

"Now? Perfect. Let's go," he said, nearly falling to the ground as he stood. It had been a minute since he'd gone on a drinking binge.

As she leaned down to catch his fall, Tony couldn't help but notice her absence of a bra. Before he knew it, his eyes and his mind had teamed up and come to the conclusion that the woman was likely, also, sans panties.

He looked down and saw that his hand was now inside hers. They were moving, and she was the one guiding him.

Alarmed voices shouted out as Tony saw a sign that said, *Women* pass in a blur. They entered the bathroom and, moments later, the accessible stall in the far corner.

She pushed him to the seat while using her free hand to undo his belt. He understood what she wanted and decided to pitch in by arching his hips and pulling his pants and boxer briefs down with a fluid tug.

Chatter abounded outside the stall. Underneath the door, a sea of legs and pumps pitter-pattered across the floor. It was after midnight and prime time in the bathroom.

She stood above him, and for a moment, he thought she would turn and leave. That would have been fine with him. He wasn't going to push it. Tony had come to the club for one reason: to hook up. But he never thought the act would be occurring on top of a public toilet. The woman had now pulled up her dress and confirmed his assumption: no panties. She stepped forward and lowered herself onto him.

Her moan echoed throughout the room as she leaned forward and gripped down, accidentally depressing the flush handle. Cold water splashed upward, spraying their naked bodies that rocked back and forth.

Cheers and shouts came from outside the stall door, and Tony looked down to see that the number of pumps had not only increased but had been joined by dozens of sneakers.

A crowd had formed in the women's bathroom, and all eyes and ears were fixed on this one stall. It was too late to stop now, but Tony didn't have to wait long. The ending came, followed by a series of victorious whoops and a few congratulations from his new fan club.

She pulled back and looked down. He put his hand to her face and directed it toward him.

"What's your name?" Tony said.

She shrugged. "Katrina," she said, almost as if she were guilty about it.

"I'm Tony," he said.

"Hello, Tony. Would you like to buy me another drink?"

He nodded.

By the time they had dressed, their audience had dispersed back into the club, where crowds of bodies were grinding in tune to a hypnotic pulse.

He grabbed her hand, pushed through to the bar, and then ordered them both mixed drinks.

"What do you see when you look in the mirror, Tony?" Katrina asked firmly without taking her eyes off him.

Tony flinched. She couldn't know about his neurotic sessions in front of the mirror.

"What are you talking about?" he asked.

She leaned forward, apparently studying his expression, and then gave him a brief smile that left her face before it truly appeared.

"I don't know what you mean," he said, downing his drink and signaling for another.

She nodded her head. "You do. You're here—probably a hundred miles from home, like me—doing this," she said, motioning to their surroundings. He said nothing but knew his eyes had spoken for him.

"What about you? What do you see when you look in the mirror?" he said uncertainly.

"A way out."

She had spoken without hesitation.

His mouth opened, but he said nothing in return.

"If you could see your face right now," Katrina said, pointing at him with a wide smile. "Come on. We're at a nightclub. Let's dance!"

She grabbed his arm and dragged him out to the sea of flailing bodies.

Chapter IV

Katrina opened the door to her apartment. The digital clock on the microwave read 7:04 a.m. She had left the club hours ago but slept in her car until she was sober enough to drive it.

She walked into her bedroom and flipped the closet light on. The mirror faced her, at attention as if it had been waiting up all night. It seemed to be jeering with an expression that said, "Didn't I tell you? There's no turning back now." And there wasn't.

Katrina went to her pantry and pulled out a paper shopping bag from the stash she kept for bi-monthly recycling. She cut the bag in half with a pair of kitchen scissors, placed it over her head, and made two small incisions on the outside of the bag at the location of each eye.

A minute later, after a few additional snips and modifications, she returned to the mirror and examined herself.

The bag had replaced her face. Two imperfectly squared holes large enough to see through stared back at her. A smile drawn from her hooker-red lipstick arched up high on both sides.

Katrina entered the closet and bent to a safe next to the mirror. She opened it and pulled out her daddy's old gun, a .45, and placed it inside a tote bag she had retrieved from the upper shelf.

She looked once more in the mirror.

The bag head was nodding.

******

Tony knew the route, the exact sequence—he knew each detail and every step necessary to execute his plan without a fault.

After his night at the club, the mental roadblock between fiction and reality had vanished. The solution to his problems had existed all along. He understood now what the mirror had been attempting to show him. They were one and the same—him and his reflection. Birds of a feather flock together.

Trust was the one thing he had been awarded for his years of service at the pharmacy. The storage unit, with boxes of supplies and refills, was under his purview. Plenty of cameras existed inside the pharmacy, but none existed within the adjacent room that held enough Oxy to kill a herd of elephants. Or enough to make Tony's pockets bulge with dough. He could sell this product for a premium to dealers from here to Chicago.

Today was his day. He would take what he wanted.

******

Katrina clutched the tote bag in one hand and gripped her pistol in the other. She showed up a minute past 8 a.m. and walked in to face Dan Stratham, who stood speaking with the other tellers about Katrina's whereabouts. She had not been late once in 15 years.

His eyes went to the gun.

"You," she said with a muffled grunt to Sabrina, a girl she knew well.

Katrina pointed to the bag.

Sabrina hesitated, but Dan spoke.

"Do it. Just do it," he said firmly.

Sabrina moved fast and began emptying each register.

There was no time to mess around with the vault in the back, but below the counter was an interim safe with at least a hundred grand.

"You," she said and pointed at Dan. "More, now," she growled.

He didn't move.

She moved quickly toward him and extended the gun to his face.

Dan's bravado had been replaced by shuddering terror. A sheen of moisture spread across his brow.

"OK—OK, let me go to the back and get," he said, holding both arms in the air.

"No," she screamed.

"OK, OK. Behind the counter," he said, bending forward and placing his hands over his head as if they would shield him from her bullets.

She tapped him on the shoulder with the muzzle and screamed, "Go."

He spun and blasted through the saloon doors that separated the main section from the space behind the counters.

Within a minute, he was back with the bag. It was filled half-way with cash.

Katrina eased toward the exit, still facing Dan, and then turned when she was outside of the building. Her car was parked in the first spot, only yards from the bank entrance. She put the gun in her tote bag, clicked the key fob, and, after a few steps, opened the SUV's door and slid into the front seat. She looked out the window to see the bank once more. Dan was now standing outside.

He looked first at the vehicle and then again at her bagged face. The terror was gone from his eyes. She had expected anger, but there was only sadness.

She looked away from him and down at her bag of cash.

This would be enough. She would leave and never return—a new start.

A new me, she thought.

*****

Tony arrived an hour before everyone else. He wasted no time and, within fifteen minutes, had loaded the back of his jeep with as much Oxy as he could get his hands on.

The Pied Piper. That's what he would be. They would be coming from all corners to find him. He would offload it all within a week and ride off into the sunset, playing music and smoking dope from here to Florida and back again to California.

Boxes and canisters were piled up on all seats.

This would be enough. He would leave and never return—a new start.

A new me, he thought.

*****

As Katrina reversed from the parking lot and turned onto the main road, she saw Dan in the rearview. He hadn't moved. She heard sirens and saw flashing lights as two cop cars pulled in beside him.

The entrance to the highway was less than half a mile ahead. She accelerated.

Thirty ... fifty ... seventy ... the SUV pushed eight-five... The light was red. She decided to push it.

And then an explosion sent her tumbling.

*****

Tony heard the sirens as he pulled out from the pharmacy.

They couldn't be here already, he thought.

But there was no time to wonder how.

He got onto the open road.

The entrance to the highway was less than half a mile ahead. He accelerated.

Thirty ... fifty ... seventy ... the Jeep pushed eight-five ... The light was red. He decided to push it.

He saw the SUV, but it was too late to stop.

His neck snapped on impact.

*****

She was surrounded by shattered glass. It was painted red and intertwined with clumps of matted hair that draped over both eyes. When Katrina heard the snap, she knew it was her neck. There had been finality in the sound.

Above her hung the rearview mirror, cracked down the middle, swinging listlessly from the battered windshield.

She thought about the night before and Tony, whom she had recognized right when she first saw him at the club. He worked at the pharmacy down the road. When he had seen her in the club, it was evident in his eyes that he had no idea who she was.

But she didn't blame him. She hadn't recognized herself either.

It's funny how life works out, she thought and coughed a final laugh.

Katrina squinted through the bloody hair that covered her face and looked into the mirror one last time.

Chapter V

"You knew them—at least one of them. Right?"

Cynthia looked up with a glower. She tilted her head and studied the stranger who stood casually above her, making presumptuous statements without preamble or introduction.

He stepped back, pulling his arms back apologetically.

"I only assumed—sorry. We don't normally cry for people we don't know. And when I say 'we,' I mean people, humans, in general. Anyway, I'm feeling stupid now," he said, offering her a hand.

The embarrassed look on his face mollified her initial exasperation. She grabbed his hand with both of hers, and he yanked her up with a single tug.

"Thanks. I knew *her*—well, I thought I did. But maybe not. At least I finally saw her in that dress I bought for her. God, that's a horrible thing to say," she said, shaking her head and gesturing toward the cops and medical personnel that had collected in the cordoned area.

"Don't be too hard on yourself. I guess you never really know anyone—only the version they are willing to show you," he said and shrugged. "Here I go again."

"During my day job, I'm a psychologist. Sometimes, I can't help but analyze everything. Ramble, ramble,

ramble," he said, chuckling to himself. His awkward demeanor was disarming. *And he's damn cute*, Cynthia thought.

"That's alright. I probably needed a little *analyzing*," she said and gave him a wink.

Here we go; now I'm flirting with him.

He nodded and said, "I'll tell you one thing: this roadblock is ruining my day. I could use a drink right now."

"God, me too. A few of them," Cynthia said.

"Oh, really? OK. Well, are you up for a little spontaneity? I know a place downtown. It's a bit of a drive the opposite way, but we sure don't seem to be going this way anytime soon. What's your trust meter saying about me right now?" he said with a mischievous smile.

"Ooh, a bit forward, aren't you?" she said, feigning surprise.

"You bet," he said. "Follow me?"

"Alright," she said and turned to open her car door.

As Cynthia settled into the front seat, she decided to check her make-up.

A cosmetic mirror rested in the cup holder. She reached over and flipped it open. Mascara ran down her face from the tears. It made her look dirty and somewhat raw. *And even a little bit sexy*, she thought.

She looked up at the handsome man waiting in front of her and then back at the mirror.

Her reflection was smiling.

The End

Deciduous

Chapter I

They are all in a room.

The distant voice filled her head, and Daisy awoke with a cry of surprise. She looked about the room before realizing, as always, that no one else was there besides Eileen, who bent down over the hospital bed with a consoling smile.

"There, there, poor girl, it's going to be OK now. You've made it through the worst of it," she said, cooing and whispering encouragement.

What Eileen said was true—Daisy had made it through the worst of it. An accident she never should have survived at all. But she had ended up in the right place at the right time during a moment that was otherwise entirely wrong.

Due to the accident, she had no complete memories of her childhood, only broken images without beginnings or endings. She recalled cloudy moments of being present but could not determine how she got there and what happened after. Most of these events involved her standing or sitting and waiting for something to occur, but what that was, she did not know.

Her only clear memory was a view of the ocean, a vast expanse of blue silver stretching toward an orange-setting sun that sank slowly and disappeared from sight. She could almost feel the cool water as she floated atop it.

The accident had occurred mid-morning on a city street in downtown. Eileen, a long-term family friend—their best friend—had been with Daisy's parents only hours before the tragedy occurred.

It was the day after high school graduation. Both mom and dad wanted to go out and celebrate, spend the day downtown, shop, eat, walk to the waterfront, and perhaps even visit the aquarium, as they used to do when she was a little girl.

Her father was driving; her mother was in the front seat. Daisy was sitting in the back. Traffic was slow due to the construction of a new skyscraper. It was set to be the tallest any United States city had seen, but no one ever got the chance to see it.

Despite a state-of-the-art plan for the superstructure, it sure didn't have a team of super employees on the job to get the work done. They messed up. And in a big way. One that cost the city its contract and the chance to make history with a generational high-rise.

As it was with all her recollections, she could only sense impressions, but this one ranked the strongest. When Eileen described what occurred, Daisy could almost see the steel girders falling from the sky, raining down on city streets.

Colossal beams of stupendous tonnage connected with vehicles, flattening them and their passengers as crowds of pedestrians were sandwiched, their heads splattering like tomatoes dropped from a thousand feet. But Daisy, the miracle girl—the one who *survived*—defied the odds and lived through it all.

When they pulled the vehicle out from the heap, her parents' bodies were no longer recognizable. The SUV had been truncated to a third of its former height. No one at ground zero bothered to look further after seeing such a mess in the front seat. It was at the scrap yard when they found her.

A manager on duty ordered the battered hunk of metal to be schlepped on top of a stack, but at the last second, a movement made him flinch. He stopped the crane operator and walked forward, and there was Daisy—trapped in the gap between the front and back seats.

Later, after extensive analysis ordered at the behest of claims adjusters and their ilk, it was determined that Daisy must have been bending down to tie her shoelace at the precise moment when the girder connected with the vehicle.

When the roof caved in, it forced her body down and, at the same time, pushed the two front seats backward, enclosing her in a cocoon-like capsule, protected from further impact. Other than an amnesia-inducing concussion, her actual physical form was unscathed.

When she arrived at the hospital, Daisy was told that her recovery process would need to be lengthy and thorough. Her condition was delicate, and any slight variance could cause a relapse. She would need to take it slow, with no sudden moves or actions that could cause a potential dive into permanent unconsciousness. It could take months. But today, after what felt more like years, Eileen gave her the good news that she had recovered in record time. She also told her something that confused her.

"It's time to get back out and do what you love, what you live for—your passion: *perform*."

Chapter II

While the words spoken by Eileen evoked no clear mental visualization, a memory of sorts was triggered by the word *perform.* A memory in her muscles. A pattern.

She couldn't recall if she knew how to drive or had ever driven but figured it was something like that. A regimen of physical actions that becomes second nature once mastered.

Daisy looked down at her body and felt a certain agility permeate as she stood on her tippy toes and spun effortlessly on the ball of one foot.

Eileen chuckled and clapped her hands.

"Very nice, *very* nice. Would it be too much to ask for a flip?" she asked, nodding indulgently.

Daisy thought about it for an instant and decided this wasn't too much to ask for at all.

She skipped nimbly to the back of the room and, without a running start of any sort, flipped forward once and then again and once more but only halfway, this time landing on her hands, perfectly erect, pausing in place as she looked around at the world from upside down.

Eileen was now jumping up and down, cheering.

"Wonderful, wonderful! Well done, my girl. You have truly recovered," she said and walked over to Daisy, who had righted herself and now faced the older woman.

Daisy looked toward the standalone mirror and ran a hand through her hair. When she woke up for the first time, she had sworn that the color of her hair had been dark brown, but then, the next time she became conscious, the color had transitioned starkly to an almost yellow-blonde. And now, with daylight pouring in from the floor-to-ceiling windows, distinct hints of red shimmered and reflected from the glass.

"Do you remember anything at all?" Eileen inquired sternly.

Daisy looked down, ashamed of the negative answer that begged to roll off her tongue.

Eileen spoke soothingly and rubbed her hand gently up and down Daisy's arm.

"It's OK, it's OK. Give it time—it will come. Everything will come."

Chapter III

Can lights shone down from suspended clamps fastened along a horizontal metal rod that ran across the length of the stage.

Daisy peered out from the far-left corridor. She could see the audience filling in. There were one, two, maybe even three thousand tiered seats, all the way up to a part of the room she knew was referred to as the nosebleed section.

Directly in front was VIP seating. Instead of stadium-style chairs, there were circular tables on top of which sat all sorts of fancy accessories and what seemed like various types of drinks and liquids in formats she had never seen before.

There was no apparent dress code for the event. Kids with baseball hats and t-shirts strolled merrily down the aisles, followed by parents with pullover sweaters and hoodies, while women in gowns and men in three-piece suits filled the orchestra pit.

"Ladies and gentlemen, the event is about to begin. Please take your seats," said a deep, welcoming voice.

Several minutes passed as the crowd settled. Meanwhile, Daisy shuddered and waited in terror.

"You're going to do great. Just do what you know, and everything will be fine," Eileen said, squeezing her hand.

Daisy nodded. She knew her routine. It had all come back to her, just as Eileen said it would. Not the memories with pictures, but the motions. However, the outfit she wore was foreign to her. She had no recollection of wearing such a tight, revealing, sleeveless onesie. The elastic quality of the material squeezed her chest together, creating a deep chasm for the world to see, while a small triangle attempted miserably to cover the vulnerable section between her legs. Her backside felt naked, with one tight strip that concealed nothing and seemed to exist only to separate the cheeks and make them more pronounced and visible.

"Ladies and gentlemen, please give a very warm welcome to your entertainer tonight, the one, the only: Daisy!" She stepped out.

The curtain rose.

And the cycle began.

Day after day, for weeks, for months, it continued without end.

Perform. Sleep. Perform. Sleep. Perform. Sleep. And each night before bed, she would look at her hair to see it morph through various shades of strawberry blonde to orange to red until, at last, on the final performance and closing night of the season, Daisy looked as if she were nearly on fire.

Vibrant curls of red-orange tumbled down her oval face and touched the swell of her voluptuous chest that paired exquisitely with an equally stunning pair of hips and perfectly curved buttocks. Her hair was not the only part of her that radiated. The rest of her body shone with a milky fluorescent light, creating a wonderful incandescence that captured thousands of scattered eyes.

As she ran, jumped, leaped, flipped, and turned, her flaming-red hair spun in a circular blur, a blaze that ripped through the air.

In the distance, from a far corner of her mind, a forgotten outpost, Daisy began to hear a voice she had heard once before—or had she heard it many times?

They are all in a room.

And that was true. This was a room, and everyone was in it.

Was that what the voice referred to?

They are all in a room.

It became louder, deafening, all-consuming, and demanding.

Daisy focused and dialed in her last shreds of concentration, channeling the voice and its desperate urgency into her final flip. With a hearty push forward on the swing, she released and launched into the air, paused momentarily in suspension, and then came down with a volley of somersaults until she landed perfectly on her feet as thunderous claps and cheers, many thousand strong, exploded from all around.

The curtains dropped, and Eileen was there, gripping Daisy's hand, but the sweat on her palm made it easy to wriggle free.

They are all in a room.

And this time, something clicked.

A combination lock had opened in her mind, and Daisy knew where she had to go.

Chapter IV

She broke away and hurtled down the steep flight of stairs, taking two at a time, ignoring Eileen's shouts to return.

They are all in a room.

It was as if a map had been etched out on the inner surface of her skull. She couldn't see it but knew instinctively what turns to make and what direction to go with the voice acting as a sonar guide.

Behind a door was a narrow hallway that led to a second door that connected to a fan of diagonal paths, each leading to its own doorway. Everything was quiet.

Eileen's footsteps had disappeared.

Daisy went forward and opened the first door. It was dark beyond the threshold. A cool breeze touched her face. She stepped forward and felt the ground beneath her sink. There was no longer vinyl tiling under her feet. She didn't need to look down to know she was walking through thick dirt and soil. Up ahead, a dim glow came from beyond a distant corner.

They are all in a room, the voice urged.

A tightly wound knot had formed in her stomach as Daisy pushed on toward the light.

In her mind, visions began to populate with each forward step she took.

The skyscraper, falling steel girders colliding with human heads as they cracked against the pavement, hot red blood, bodies– heaps and heaps of bodies

And then another set of images—different yet somehow the same. But before they could play out fully in her mind, she stepped into the room and saw them in real life.

A cylindrical, tree-like stalk of metal rose high into the air, its trunk mired in soiled ground. Studded bulbs ran up and down the length of thick, wiry branches that shot from all directions. In her mind, many images appeared of giant oaks, willows, and maples, lifeless and naked during winter months, but this one, directly in front of her, looked very much alive. It was breathing, pulsating.

She stepped forward, and a crunching sound stopped her heart. Daisy looked down and saw three bony fingers protruding from below her left shoe.

They are all in a room, the voice said, and this time with conviction. As in, *and now you see.*

Daisy recoiled and tripped over something solid as she stumbled back and fell to the ground.

They were everywhere. Thrown on top of each other, piled in mounds, some partially submerged in the dirt, sinking slowly, decomposing, and transitioning gradually into human mulch.

Each body was identical: an hourglass figure, an oval face, hazel eyes, and a head full of long, bright, vibrant red hair.

They were all duplicates of her. Thousands of them scattered about the room.

The dead eyes that stared back at her were frightening, but even worse were the ones that still blinked, their bodies partially submerged as if they were stuck in quicksand and had no other choice but to wait stoically until the end finally came.

Daisy turned and ran.

Chapter V

Her heart pounded as she ran on rubber legs, struggling to retrace her steps without a vocal guide to direct her. She had left the place she was meant to remain forever.

Up ahead was the long hallway. She could hear voices and laughter echoing. A little girl with platinum blonde hair and a pink dress walked out from behind a door. She stopped, cocked her head, and pointed to Daisy.

"Red means dead," she said sweetly.

Laughter danced in her sparkling green eyes as she spun on one heel and scampered off, chanting and singing.

"Red means dead! Red means dead! Red means dead!"

Before Daisy could move, Eileen came from behind the door and pulled her in.

"You aren't supposed to be here. Come with me," she said, her face ashen.

Daisy followed as they moved along a circuit of hallways, down a flight of stairs, and through several doors that eventually led to an empty room. She turned and faced Eileen.

"I saw everything. They were all me, all together, and all dying. Something is happening to me. I can't explain it. I feel like I'm fading," Daisy said, breathing heavily.

Eileen placed her hands on Daisy's shoulders and looked at her sympathetically. "How much do you know about nature and flora?"

Daisy scrunched her forehead.

"Oh, you know—trees, plants, bushes. All that wonderful lush foliage that abounds here in this beautiful country," Eileen said, gesticulating with one hand.

"I guess I'm not sure. I don't know much about that at all. Other than the colors. Some are green, but others change and become quite beautiful."

A knowing look spread across Eileen's face, and she nodded slowly.

"Correct."

In the room of horror, adrenaline had subdued Daisy's anxiety, but now latent dread and terror had taken over. She felt alone in a dark forest. One where monstrous beasts lurked and masqueraded as guardians of the land, only to swoop in at the final moment to consume their prey.

Beasts like Eileen.

"Who are you?" Daisy asked with a trembling voice.

Eileen sighed.

"That's not the real question you want an answer for, is it?" she asked with a quarter smile. "You want to know who *you* are. Am I right?" Eileen finished.

Daisy felt light-headed. If she fainted now, she knew she would never wake up again.

"The answer is in the question I asked you about nature. Have you ever wondered why water and sunlight are the only things you require as sustenance? I know you don't interact with many people, but I'm sure you have seen some of them insert a solid substance into their mouths. That's called food. I know you can't smell, but you've seen it."

Daisy considered this. She had never questioned needing anything other than water and sunlight. But on event nights, through the mist and footlights, she did recall how the audience below her sat with circles in front of them, and upon these circles were items that people placed in their mouths. She had assumed this was a fancy way of consuming water, perhaps via an ingestible carrier that dissolved on contact.

Eileen placed an arm around her.

"I have not told others this. I guess I've never felt the urge. Perhaps that makes me and everyone involved in this exhibitionist game—well, I don't know—monsters."

"I don't understand," Daisy said. Her eyes prickled, and she could feel the moisture as tears balled up and began to fall down her cheeks.

"How could you?" Eileen said kindly. "You were never meant to. It was not part of your programming to understand. Just as nature has forests of trees, science has forests of its own. Only you are not the tree, dear. You are the leaf. And leaves on deciduous trees transform into a brilliance of color but die at their peak of beauty and fall to the ground. As will you, I'm afraid, in only a matter of hours."

Daisy wiped the tears and looked away.

"My parents, the accident—was it all a lie?" she said, looking up at Eileen, who shrugged.

"It depends on how you view it. What is a lie—how do you even exist? One could say that you are a lie, Daisy. An entity fronting as a human," she said softly, matter-of-factly, but with no cruelty in her voice. "You are a child of science and genetic coding, brought into existence and housed inside a form of vegetation that I can't even begin to understand. You are not a real girl. But you *are* different from the rest. None before you have asked questions or even doubted their place in this world."

Daisy shook her head. Her fear had transformed into rage. "I am real. As real as you. And I will not end in that room. Discarded. Like garbage. Waiting for the Earth to swallow me as I still breathe." She paused and stared at her fraudulent foster parent. "So, you are going to let me go."

Eileen tilted her head and narrowed her eyes. Her face showed indecision with an underlying tone of curiosity. She looked searchingly at Daisy and then up to the ceiling, as if pondering the consequences of setting her free. And then she extended an arm and pointed to the door.

Chapter VI

Daisy was unsure what to expect but assumed guards or a gate would block her exit. These terms existed in her vocabulary and seemed to pair well with circumstances relating to escape. As she walked past Eileen and out the door, however, no one and nothing was blocking her way.

The woman could have pointed out many other ways that all might have led elsewhere. Daisy couldn't help but think Eileen had planned it this way. Ahead was the forest. Fall's end had arrived and blanketed the ground with leaves that would soon become mulch and a part of Earth's cycle of rebirth and growth.

She picked up her pace to a light jog and noticed that her breathing improved with each step. It had not occurred to her until now that the further she got from the room—*from the superstructure*—the better she felt.

Her jog turned into a sprint, and she zig-zagged through the trees, her feet pounding into the dirt, crunching leaves into pieces as they leapt up in her wake. Ahead of her, the flat terrain transitioned into a decline, revealing a horizon and the ocean, a vast expanse of blue-silver stretching out and beyond.

The sun hung for a moment and paused as if it had been waiting for her to arrive before the last bit of orange sank and disappeared into the sea.

The End

What's on the Menu?

Chapter I

"Chris, *Chris*! What do you think it's going to be?" Jesse said, looking up at him, her eyes filled with envy. "Oh, what's it going to be, Chris? Can't you take me with you, *please*? Pretty, *pretty*, please?"

Chris Newberry picked up his little sister and held her high in the air. She squealed gleefully as he spun her around until they both swayed with dizziness.

"I don't know, Marge," he said, lowering her back to the ground. "I really don't. They told me nothin', I swear. I'd tell you if they did—even though I'm not supposed to say anything about it."

"I'm going out to play. I can't wait to tell all my friends how famous my older brother is," she said and ran out the door.

Chris fell back onto a tattered sofa. He rested his head against the worn armrest and closed his eyes. Mental images of fried chicken, roast beef sandwiches, juicy cheeseburgers, and other delicacies floated majestically in a sea of delight and wonder.

The pill was the only form of sustenance he had ever known. One a day was all it took.

They called it *regulating*. Two cups of water were recommended to allow complete release and absorption.

The pill was tasteless, but the subsequent burps had a different flavor each time. It was enough to provide a hint of how food had once tasted.

There was no way to tell how long life had been this way. As far as Chris knew, not a single Newberry, going back hundreds of years, had ever consumed actual food.

Not until now. Or at least, *soon to be now.*

It was so close he could taste it, Chris thought and chuckled. And how appropriate that statement was.

Tomorrow was going to be a big day.

Chapter II

A jolt and then a series of bangs ripped him from his reverie. Chris shot up and stumbled toward a rattling front door that was hanging on by one last rusty hinge.

Jacob and three others rushed in. They surrounded him from all sides.

"Chris, man, we were down at the dispensary, picking up our weekly rations, and what I heard—I cannot believe it. Everyone is talking about it: your mom, your dad, all sixteen of your cousins, man. I can't effing believe it. One in whatever billion chance and—*is it true*? Did you actually win the lottery?" he said, shouting the last question.

Chris shrugged. A goofy smile spread across his broad face.

Jacob swooped in, wrapped both arms around his waist, and attempted to hoist him upward. But despite being raised on food supplements alone, Chris was a big boy with big bones. He was well beyond a size that Jacob could handle alone. The other boys took his struggle as their cue and pitched in, grabbing a fistful of whatever they could get a hold of, and placed Chris on their shoulders as if they had just won a national title and he was the MVP.

After a series of chants, they tossed him onto the couch and got down on their knees in front of him, each gaze locked in and riveted on the wonder of Chris Newberry. A hailstorm of questions commenced.

"So, what's it going to be?"

"Will there be steak? A whole cow? A pig with an apple in its mouth? A stuffed turkey?"

"Dessert? Will you have dessert, Chris? Chocolate cake with strawberries, whipped cream, and ice cream on the side with caramel sauce and shaved nuts, drizzled with pineapple jelly, and hot fudge with a cherry on top?"

The boys worked themselves into a dither as they fantasized about endless possibilities.

"I heard about the last sitting," said Jacob, and all necks snapped toward him.

"Well, not directly," he said confidentially. "But I heard rumors."

"Did you see pictures?" one boy whispered.

"Of course not, you idiot—you know the penalty for that," hissed Jacob. "But I heard of a beef stew. A gorgeous, delicious stew with potatoes and carrots and tender hunks of aged steak that came from grass-fed cattle. And—*and*," he emphasized, pausing for impact, "a brisket smoked so long the meat melted the instant it hit your tongue."

The boys, Chris included, stared wondrously at Jacob and hung desperately on each romantic word that fell from his mouth.

He then looked toward Chris and spoke solemnly.

"Now that one of us has been picked, I'd like to enact our former pact," he said. His voice was stern but vibrated anxiously. Chris knew what he had just proposed was tantamount to high treason, as was their initial pact.

"This goes for all of us," he said, making the rounds, staring into each of their stony faces. "And I know if one of you disagrees, it could mean my life. That is a risk I am willing to take."

Each boy nodded and, without speaking, placed their hands one on top of the other, forming a stack of ten.

"I promise."
"I promise."
"I promise."

Chris looked at Jacob, who kept his cool but couldn't prevent a bead of sweat from rolling down his angular face. The other boys looked at Chris pleadingly.

"I promise, too," he said and sighed.

Several years ago, after completing their term of standard schooling, they had all formally agreed about how they would handle it if one of them ever won *What's on the Menu?*

What's on the Menu? was the reason they lived—the reason anyone lived. It was the national lottery—the one game, contest, sporting event, and any other type of entertainment all packaged together. There was nothing else.

This was what their meager paychecks went toward after the bulk was spent on housing, food supplements, water, and supporting the International Army that kept the rest of the world at bay.

Each house had a TV, and on this TV, the only thing that played were interviews of past lottery winners who spoke about the magic of *What's on the Menu?* Pictures of food that had lived only in centuries that were long dead and gone—perfectly grilled cuts of meat, deluxe arrangements of fruit, street tacos, fondue, slices of pizza oozing with crisp bubbly cheese, cinnamon rolls with frosting dripping down the sides, foot-long chocolate bars with almonds and chunks of toffee jutting from the edges, and on and on and on, never-ending torturous images scrolling on a carousel that was unrelenting and impossibly out of reach to all who stood by watching, wishing, drooling, each of them knowing they would likely never have a chance to experience such divinity for as long as they drew breath within their pathetically pointless span of time on Earth.

They showed real-life footage of the last animals being kept alive by proceeds of the lottery, raised on acres of fertile land where they bred, grazed, and prepared themselves for slaughter to be fed to the lucky winners of *What's on the Menu?*

Chris looked down at Jacob and the other members of his illicit crew.

"As agreed years before, I promise, following my return from *What's on the Menu?* to describe, without omission of one single detail, the complete experience from beginning to end. Every dish served, each bite I consume, any drink I imbibe, and all smells and tactile sensations will be relayed so you can experience the event vicariously through me. I promise this on my life."

Tears began to cascade down Jacob's face.

"It's the best we can ask for, boys," he said between sobs. "One of us gets in. But *all* of us get to live it," he said with gusto.

They murmured sounds of agreement and nodded their heads furiously. One boy thrust his arm into the air with a clenched fist.

"And I'm just glad it's you, mate," Jacob continued, placing a hand on Chris' shoulder.

"'Cause I'm crap at telling stories. If it were me, I'd come back and tell you all I ate like a wild hog and forget all the details. And you all would kill me where I stand for not properly relaying the experience of a lifetime."

An abrupt statement from Chris snuffed out the gale of laughter that followed.

"Alright. Out. Now. Everyone. I have to get ready," he said, and his friends were on their feet, nodding, saluting, and showering him with *Yes, Sir, right away, of course, we're leaving now, Godspeed, see you after the weekend, don't forget about us, you are our Messiah, bring us home Lord.*

Once Chris shut the door on the last of them and had all 220 square feet of his one-room bungalow to himself, he switched on the TV and scrolled to a tab that read *Winner Preparation Presentation.* He inserted two earbuds, took a pair of elastic-banded goggles from the charging console, strapped them over his eyes, and did up the clasp at the back of his head.

A female voice spoke from the buds:

Stand and scan the room for verification of no human presence.

A pie chart appeared on the screen. It began to fill as he turned around the room. Once he had peered under the couch, inserted his head inside every cabinet, and practically dived into the toilet bowl, he got confirmation that the space was now clear.

Your Winner Preparation Presentation video will start now. Warning: Remain perfectly still throughout your viewing. Any extraneous sounds, as much as a single cough, will cause the video stream to cease and may invoke a disqualification event.

A terror unlike that he had ever sensed radiated down his spine and made his toes curl. *Jesse, don't even think about entering now. Please, I'm begging you.*

His sister was the only one who made random appearances after hours. Yet these were not ordinary times—anyone was bound to appear now.

Anyone.

Bold text appeared on the screen, and Chris saw his fear had been uncalled for:

Start of Winner Preparation Presentation.
Be outside at dawn for pick-up.
End of Winner Preparation Presentation.

An image of two lamb chops appeared, and the carousel resumed its regular beat.

Chris drew a deep breath of relief. He had never experienced such tension. His knees were still locked—a mess of anxiety-induced hormones pooled inside his stomach.

Black splotches and what seemed to be an army of floaters crowded his vision and impeded the view of what was now a smiling blonde promoting the humanitarian virtues of *What's on the Menu?*

And better still, each dollar you spend goes directly toward pre-serving man-kind, she said. The final two words dragged slowly from her mouth, with elongated syllables inflected to comical proportions.

Chris watched her lips turn up, up, and up until the smile was so wide it appeared to reach the bottom of her ear lobes, and then darkness took over as consciousness departed.

Blinding pain brought him back.

He opened his eyes, expecting to see someone above him with a gnarled club or a wooden board, but no one was present.

It took a moment to register what happened, but eventually, he got there: Chris had forgotten to regulate—no wonder he had felt woozy. The pain had been caused by his head connecting with a wooden floor plank. He pushed himself up and stumbled toward the counter, where his seven-day pill case rested.

After fifteen minutes and two glasses of water, he felt much better. His senses were rejuvenated, and life looked right.

There was now nothing but a few ticks of the clock between him and history.

Chapter III

Chris fought heavy eyelids as he blinked at first light. He had been outside waiting on his front steps since night fell to prevent any risk of sleeping in. A miss at this opportunity would have thrown him into an emotional chasm from which he could never have climbed up from.

He had intended not to sleep at all, but the witching hours took their toll, and now, although dawn was here, no golden chariot awaited.

He had never been capable of much imagination but was considering now the possibility of being escorted in a fancy car or maybe even a limousine with tinted windows and a minibar.

Or even a backseat filled with scantily dressed girls. That was pushing it. But a boy could dream.

Instead, he had awoken to cold, sheer panic. What if this was a mistake? Or worse, a *prank*. The trite old saying had come through: it was too good to be true.

"Chris Newberry?" said a voice with an oddly familiar timbre. Chris had heard such an accent before, perhaps in an old movie—one that was played at school during history class.

"Yeah," Chris said and looked up at the man who stood next to what looked like a real-life, legitimate taxi cab—a yellow sedan with black lettering. It was identical to the ones he had seen in pictures on the streets of ancient cities such as New York and Chicago.

"Jesus, pal, you gonna stare at me foreva'? Let's go, move it!" He snapped and threw open the back door of the cab.

"But where are we going?" Chris said.

The man turned slowly and faced Chris. "Well, hell, it's a good thing wits aren't no qualification to be a winna, eh?" he said and paused.

Chris felt as if he had lost the ability to speak. His tongue was a frigid slab of steel. He stared densely at the man.

"Are you comin' to *What's on the Menu?* or not?" he shouted, emphasizing his point with a thump of his fist on the car door.

For the second time in twenty-four hours, Chris found himself flat on the ground as he attempted to burst forward and dive into the backseat but instead made it no further than the bottom of his front steps.

"Bloody Jesus, Mary, Joseph, and all the frickin' saints. Get the hell up, pal!" the man said, standing above Chris with one arm extended.

Chris grabbed the man's hand and pulled himself up, and a minute later, they were hurtling down the road in the yellow cab.

"Gotta do this, pal, sorry—confidential location and all. But you'll be up in no time," the man said.

Chris, who had been gazing out the window, looked toward the front seat. The man was holding an atomizer. It looked like an old perfume bottle. He depressed it three times, and everything went black.

Chapter IV

"Alright, sleepy-head, the moment has come—the moment has come."

Gusts of cool air licked his face. Chris wanted to open his eyes, but they seemed glued shut.

"Just give it a minute. It's powerful stuff. Walkin' around helps; let's go," the man said. Chris sat up and groped for the handle, but before he could get a hold of it, the car door swung open, and a network of hands yanked him to his feet.

"Chris Newberry, welcome!" a voice said.

A splash of water, more like a bucket load, doused him at face level. Two muscular bodies frog-marched him toward what he could now see was a front door. Chris saw something else as well: miraculously, in some way, he had been transported back in time. Or, more likely—due to the impossibility of time travel—he had been lied to his entire life. But it didn't matter. What he saw was incredible.

Skyscrapers towered above him. Fancy shops lined the boulevard, teamed with businessmen and classy women in fur coats who each walked purposefully, crossing streets filled with luxury vehicles. Neon signs with pictures and names of entertainers and brands lit up the twilight sky.

"Now you've seen it—let's go, time for the real party," one of the men said, pushing Chris through the two open doors leading to a room with vaulted ceilings.

Laughter and frenetic chatter echoed and rebounded off the walls. Trays with bubbly drinks in elegant flutes passed through the room on the outstretched arms of blonde, brunette, and red-haired beauties in black, tight mini-skirts. Pockets of billowing cigar and cigarette smoke were scattered about, surrounded by sharply dressed men adorned with pocket watches and silk handkerchiefs.

Chris felt devastatingly under-dressed in a pair of old jeans and a tattered white t-shirt. The other guests wore gowns, black tuxedos, or tricked-out suits.

"My name is Adrian. I will be at your side throughout this event. And don't worry, you will be dressed soon," he said.

Chris reached out to shake Adrian's hand, but the man extended an over-filled flute and said, "Drink. Be merry."

Floral-scented liquid dribbled down the side of the glass and fell onto his forearm. Chris stuck out his tongue and licked it. A burst of flavor enveloped his tongue. It tingled. This was his first taste of anything at any time—besides the faint hints of flavor from burps. "You will like it better if you drink from the glass," Adrian said with an indulgent smile.

"Go on—it's *champagne*."

Chris took a deep sip and watched the glass empty past the halfway mark. A powerful sensation rose from his stomach and crashed onto his senses as everything surrounding him began to tilt.

Adrian grabbed his arm and directed him toward an empty table. "The winner's circle," he said with a flourish.

"Am I the first one?" Chris asked.

Adrian raised his eyebrows. "Enjoy the show; I will return shortly," he said, turned, and disappeared.

For a country boy who had seen nothing but barren land, concrete, and wooden shacks for his two decades on Earth, the commotion that faced Chris was overwhelming.

In addition to the mingling guests, preparations for the feast were being carried out in a hot frenzy. Servers readied a large banquet table with a white tablecloth and fine porcelain plates with ornate silverware off to the side. Individual stations were being established along the walls with mounds of watermelon, pears, peaches, plums, and enormous chocolate fountains that flowed into pools next to beds of strawberries.

A smoker was directly in front of him, so close he could reach out and touch it. At least, that's what he believed it was. He had seen plenty of photos and videos of similar units.

Although the ones he had seen were relatively small—wide enough to fit a small roast or perhaps a turkey. This one was large enough to fit an entire hog, maybe two.

This was all living up to the rumors he had heard about the meal being prepared and cooked within sight.

Chris hoped the festivities would start soon. His stomach was grumbling.

Adrian had appeared again. He held something in his hand.

"A copy of tonight's menu, Sir. Oh, and as promised, your dressing will commence soon," he said with a wry smile.

Chris took it and unsnapped a button that joined two delicate sections of parchment. He looked down and began to read.

It didn't take him long.

What's on the Menu?
Featured entree: Chris Newberry—dressed and marinated in a blend of exotic herbs and spices, slow-roasted

Around him, the commotion had ceased. There was no movement or sound of any sort.

All that remained was thick, hungry silence.

Chris raised his head.

A room of carnivorous eyes stared back at him.

The End